CALPURNIA TATE · GIRL VET

SKUNKED!

BY **JACQUELINE KELLY**

WITH ILLUSTRATIONS BY **JENNIFER L. MEYER**

HENRY HOLT AND COMPANY · NEW YORK

HENRY HOLT AND COMPANY

Publishers since 1866

175 Fifth Avenue

New York, New York 10010

mackids.com

Library of Congress Cataloging-in-Publication Data

Names: Kelly, Jacqueline, author.

Title: Skunked!: Calpurnia Tate, girl vet / Jacqueline Kelly.

Description: First edition | New York : Henry Holt and Company, 2016. |

Series: Calpurnia Tate, Junior Veterinarian

Identifiers: LCCN 2015041958 (print) | LCCN 2016008077 (ebook) | ISBN

9781627798686 (hardback) | ISBN 9781627798693 (Ebook)

Subjects: | CYAC: Skunks—Infancy—Fiction. | Naturalists—Fiction. |

Veterinarians—Fiction. | Family life—Texas—Fiction. |

Texas—History—1846–1950—Fiction. | BISAC: JUVENILE FICTION / Animals /

General. | JUVENILE FICTION / Historical / United States / 20th Century.

Classification: LCC PZ7.K296184 Tr 2016 (print) | LCC PZ7.K296184 (ebook) |

DDC [Fic]—dc23

LC record available at http://lccn.loc.gov/2015041958

Our books may be purchased in bulk for promotional, educational,

or business use. Please contact your local bookseller or the Macmillan

Corporate and Premium Sales Department at (800) 221-7945 ext. 5442

or by e-mail at MacmillanSpecialMarkets@macmillan.com.

First edition—2016 / Designed by April Ward

Printed in the United States of America by

R. R. Donnelley & Sons Company, Harrisonburg, Virginia

1   3   5   7   9   10   8   6   4   2

For animal lovers everywhere

None of the terrible things that [4 problem] happened need have happened at all if the skunk hadn't drawn atten- [Why they so] tion to itself by ripping up our garden and stealing a bunch of vegetables. And if Father hadn't told the hired man to set a trap and kill it. And if the skunk

hadn't turned out to be a mother with a baby hidden in a den nearby. And if my younger brother Travis hadn't heard the hungry baby crying and stopped to investigate.

But this unfortunate chain of events did occur, with Travis winding up in disgrace and a hero at the exact same time.

You may wonder how one boy, age

eleven and a half, could end up both heroic and disgraced on the same day. Well, I'm going to tell you about it, and it's all true. There may be some people in our town of Fentress, Texas, who suspect me of stretching the truth from time to time, but I swear this is not one of those times.

In 1901 we lived in a big white house near the San Marcos River: me, Mother, Father, Granddaddy, and a total of six brothers. How I got stuck in this big old mess of boys I'll never know. Life is just not fair sometimes. Rivers tend to attract wildlife, so living near a river is an excellent thing if you happen to be interested in such. Travis and I were both interested in wildlife but for different reasons. I was interested because Granddaddy was teaching me Science. Together we studied all kinds of life, wild and tame, big and small, flora and fauna (meaning both plants and animals). Travis, on the other hand, was crazy about animals as pets. He was always bringing home some wild creature or other, determined to make it his pet. He persisted in doing this even when the creature was just as determined to *not* be his pet.

One fine day in May, he went down to the river. On the way he heard a strange noise unlike anything he'd ever heard before. The noise was like a squeak and a hiss and a grumble all mixed up together.

"Hello?" he said. "Who's there?"

The noise stopped. Some other boy might have been scared, but Travis knew these woods and was not afraid. He stood very still. Then he heard the noise again. It was coming from a hollow tree. He peered inside and saw a tiny animal looking up at him.

"A kitten! How'd you get stuck in

there? Don't worry. I'll get you out, and then I'll help you look for your mama."

Travis reached in. He gently pulled the kitten out. Except that the warm furry body curled in his palm wasn't a kitten. It was a kit. Also known as a baby skunk.

Travis nearly dropped the kit in shock. But he knew that skunks spray only when they are scared or upset, so he stood very still and made no sound. He and the kit stared at each other. The baby had shiny black eyes, two white stripes down its back, and a fluffy tail. It sniffed his hand and tried to nibble his thumb.

"Poor little guy, I guess you're hungry. Where's your mama? We better find her." He explored the surrounding woods for a while, but there was no sign of her.

Finally he said, "I guess I have to take you home with me. Your mama's not going to be happy, and my mama's not going to be happy, either. She doesn't like it when I bring wild animals home, although I don't see anything wrong with it myself. I'll have to hide you somewhere or she'll pitch a fit."

The kit began to squirm and grumble, so Travis tucked it into the bib of his overalls, where it settled right down. (It's a cruel world for orphaned skunks unless they have the great good fortune of meeting my brother.)

"All right, let's get you to your new home."

The kit stayed quiet while Travis fretted about hiding it from Mother.

"I guess you'll have to live in the chicken coop." He thought about this for a minute. "I suspect the chickens won't like that. They're really fussy. You won't believe the racket they make when someone goes in their pen, even to feed them. And I can't put you in the root cellar. Our cook, Viola, goes in there all the time to fetch potatoes. So I guess it's the barn for you, my friend."

If the kit had any thoughts about this, he kept them to himself.

Travis sneaked into the barn. He hurried past the horses and the milk cow and the barn cats to the farthest corner, where he kept his tame rabbits. It was dark and gloomy back there, and a new addition to the family would be less likely to be noticed. He hoped.

He spoke to his prizewinning

Angora rabbit. "Bunny, I want you to meet your new friend."

He held the skunk up to Bunny's cage. Bunny's nose twitched once; the kit's nose twitched once. And then they ignored each other. So much for new friends.

Viola rang the dinner bell on the back porch. Travis shoved the kit into the empty cage next to Bunny's, saying, "Mother gets upset if we're late to the table. After we eat, I'll bring you your dinner, once I figure out what that is, of course."

He hurried inside and took his place next to me at the long table crammed with hungry brothers. After the blessing, he whispered, "Say, Callie, what do skunks eat?"

I gave him a wary look. "Why do you ask?"

"Um, no reason. I'm just curious."

He went back to eating his ham and potatoes and pretended not to notice that I was now staring at him in alarm.

"Travis," I hissed, "tell me you didn't."

"Didn't what?"

"Tell me you didn't bring a skunk home," I said, trying to whisper, but I was so anxious it came out a sort of strangled whisper-scream.

Mother said, "Is there something wrong? Do you two have something you wish to share with the rest of us?"

"No, Mother," we said, and stared at our plates.

Later when Mother was busy talking

to someone else, I whispered to him,
"There's no skunk, right?"

He didn't answer.

"Right?"

He didn't speak. He didn't need to. I
could see the answer in his face.

After dinner Travis grabbed a paring knife and stole an apple from the pantry and ran to the barn. The kit stood on his hind legs when he saw Travis and tried to reach through the wire with his paws.

"Don't worry. I haven't forgotten

about you. Look, I brought you
an apple. I hope you like it."

He was so busy slicing it that he
didn't hear me sneak up behind him.

"Idiot!" I cried, and he jumped about
a foot in the air.

After landing back on earth, he said,
"Gosh, Callie, you scared the life out of

me. And it's not very nice of you to call me an idiot."

"I'm calling you an idiot for the simple reason that you are one. Nobody in their right mind brings a skunk home. Can you imagine what Mother and Father will say? You've got to let it go this instant before it sprays someone."

The baby grumbled and reached for the apple.

"Look, Callie, he's hungry. We have to at least feed him."

Travis unlatched the cage and held out a slice of apple. The starving kit took it in its tiny paws and ate the whole thing in five seconds flat. Then, with

twitching nose, it held out its paws for more.

It really was very cute. And it didn't seem to smell. And normally no one visited this corner of the barn except Travis. And owls and coyotes hunted nearby at night. And that's why I agreed, against my better judgment, to keep it overnight and let it go "first thing in the morning." (This makes *me* such an idiot I can barely believe it.)

By the time morning came, Travis had named the kit Stinky, which wasn't strictly true.

Let me tell you something you might not know: The rule is that once you've made the mistake of yanking a wild animal out of its natural habitat, you have to look after it. You become responsible for its welfare. And once you've given it a name? It's all over. That animal becomes part of your family. So although Travis looked like the same brother on the outside, inside he had turned into a mama skunk.

The next day was Saturday. Travis and I zipped out to the barn before dawn to check on the baby. We fed it some carrot peelings, and it gobbled them down so fast I was afraid it would choke.

"All right," I said, "that's done. I'm

going out now to make my Scientific Observations. You can come too but you have to be quiet. You know how you are." Travis tended to chatter while I was working, and oftentimes I had to shush him to get my work done.

Travis scooped up the kit and stuffed him down his overalls.

"What are you doing?" I said.

"I'm bringing Stinky along for the walk."

"Don't be silly."

Travis peeked down his bib. "Look, he's asleep. He won't be any trouble, I promise."

I looked, and the kit had indeed fallen fast asleep against Travis's chest. It looked a whole lot happier than me. I sighed. What could you do with a brother like this?

"Okay. But if I hear a single peep out of either one of you, you're on your own. Got it?"

"Got it." He smiled.

On the way to the river, he proceeded to tell me a long, complicated story about something that had happened at school between him and my best friend, Lula, and I had to shush him about twelve times. Each time he'd nod and promise to be quiet, and then a minute later he'd be gabbing again. Normally I enjoyed his company, but not when I was working. My observations were serious stuff.

We made it to the inlet and found a good place to sit on the riverbank just as the sun was coming up through the trees. The water at the inlet was quiet and shallow. It didn't smell so good, but it was an excellent place to find turtles and tadpoles and such. Travis lay back on the warming grass and snoozed. I printed in my Scientific Notebook: *May 20. Clear and fine. Winds from*

the southwest. Then I sat quietly and waited for Nature to show herself to me.

A few minutes later, a great blue heron glided silently down the river and, to my great surprise, landed in the shallows only twenty feet away. It had not noticed us. I froze in place and prayed that Travis would stay still. I'd never seen the *Ardea herodias* up close before. The bird was huge, with a wing-span of six feet, its beak long and sharp as a dagger, its plumage a mixture of rich blue and gray. Suddenly, faster than my eye could follow, it snaked its head into the water and came up with a

small perch. Was the fish
for its own breakfast
or was it intended
for its hatch-
lings? Maybe
there was a nest
nearby. Herons
built nests that
looked like huge
piles of sticks all
jumbled up, so
messy that you
wondered how
they held together.

Just then the kit stirred and woke

Travis, who started to sit up. I hissed at him, "Shh, don't move," but it was too late. The heron launched itself into the air with a harsh cry of outrage, so at odds with its graceful appearance. It flew downriver with ponderous wing-beats, each flap so slow it made you wonder how it could possibly stay aloft.

"Wow," said Travis. He saw the look on my face and said, "Sorry, Callie, I didn't mean to scare it off."

But I was too busy looking at what the bird had left behind to chew him out properly. In the shallows floated a large blue feather, almost a foot long. I hurried to snag it with a stick before it floated away. I ended up getting my boots wet but it was worth it. Holding it to the sun, I noticed it looked blue when I turned it one way and gray when I turned it the other. Why? I'd have to ask Granddaddy about this.

I let Travis hold it for a minute to let him know I'd forgiven him.

"It's a real beauty," he said. "Are you going to make a pen out of it?"

I was tempted, but

33

quill pens were hard to use without making a terrible mess everywhere. Pencils were much safer. I said, "No, I think I'll just add it to my shelf." I kept a collection of bones and fossils and other such treasures in my room. "And besides," I went on, "my penmanship is nothing to write home about."

I watched him to see if he got the joke. It took him a moment, but then he laughed. I always enjoyed making him laugh. It was like the sun bursting out from behind the clouds on a gloomy day.

We made our way toward the cotton

gin. Halfway there, Stinky poked his head out and started making loud grumble-squeaks.

"What's wrong with him?" I said.

"I don't know. He looks okay to me. Maybe he's hungry again."

We entered a clearing, and the kit got louder and louder, its calls echoing from tree to tree. I listened closely.

"What is that?" I said. By now the skunk was squawking so loudly you could barely hear yourself think.

Travis looked puzzled. Then he broke into a big smile and trotted over to a hollow tree. He peered inside and said, "Look, Callie! It's the tree where I found Stinky."

I looked. To Travis's joy—and to my dismay—a pair of tiny black button eyes gleamed faintly in the dark.

Another kit.

"Oh boy, another one!" Travis cried, all excited. Stinky grew even more excited at being reunited with his brother (or sister, who could tell?). The three of them would have thrown a party if I'd let them. The only one not excited by the reunion was yours truly. No, not excited. Not at all.

Stinky wriggled and would have fallen to the ground but for Travis catching him just in time. "Here," he said, shoving him at me.

"Uh, I don't think—" But it was too late. I was left holding one kit while Travis practically dived into the hollow tree for the other. To my surprise, Stinky was soft and warm and furry, and he didn't smell. He tickled as he sniffed my fingers. I hated to admit it, but he was really kind of . . . cute.

Travis emerged with the other kit. It squirmed feebly in his hand. It was only half the size of Stinky, but it looked about two-thirds dead to me.

"Oh, Travis," I said, knowing the heartbreak that lay ahead, "it's the runt of the litter. It isn't going to make it. You should put it back."

He looked aghast. "We can't just leave it here. We have to try. You have to help me."

I thought for a moment. Did I dare go to the vet, Dr. Pritzker? It would be asking a lot. He didn't look after wild animals, especially wild animals like skunks that were considered the lowest of the low. They were varmints and pests, real nuisances to the local farmers, tearing up gardens and stealing eggs from the henhouse. Nobody in town would ever dream of trying to save a skunk because they were all too busy trying to kill them. Dr. Pritzker might think I was crazy or—much worse—stupid. And I didn't want him to think I was crazy or stupid, because he sometimes let me watch him doctor the cattle and horses, useful animals that were actually worth something. All that would come to a sudden halt if he thought I was crazy or stupid. I weighed all these things up. Then my soft-hearted brother began to plead with me.

"Please, Callie, we have to try.

Please." He looked so upset that I knew I'd have to give in.

I sighed. He cracked a huge smile, knowing he'd won me over.

I shoved Stinky at him and said, "See if you can get some food into the little one. I'll go to Dr. Pritzker's and meet you at home."

"Thanks! You won't regret it." He jogged off, clutching the kits to him.

"Of course I will," I shouted at him. "I always do!" Then I took off in the other direction. I made the run downtown to Dr. Pritzker's office in record time, and I was relieved to see his mare,

Penny, hitched to his buggy out front.
I'd caught him before he left on his first
call of the day.

I didn't even stop to give Penny her
usual pat on the nose but burst through
the door, startling the doctor who was
looking over some papers on his desk.

"What is it, Calpurnia? What's the
trouble?"

I paused to catch my breath and think. I couldn't tell him we had a skunk. So I said, "Dr. Pritzker, I'm worried about one of our, uh, kittens. It's awfully small, it's the runt of the litter, and I told my brother we should just let it go, but he wants to try and save it."

"Do you think that's a good idea? Nature doesn't usually intend the runts to live."

"I know, but Travis has his heart set on trying. What should we do?"

"Well, the first thing you have to do is keep it warm somehow. Once they lose body heat, they start to fail quickly. And it needs to feed frequently. Is the mother cat around to feed it?"

"She's . . . gone."

"Is it old enough to eat solid food? Some ground-up meat?"

"Uh, maybe not. It looks pretty weak to me."

"Then you'll have to feed it milk somehow, either with a sponge it can suck on or with a very small bottle. And you'll need to warm the milk first."

"Okay, I will. Is there anything else we can do?"

"You can hope for the best. And I do

hope you and Travis won't feel too badly if it dies. Runts often do, even when you do everything to save them."

"Thank you."

I dashed back out. It wasn't until I'd got most of the way home and saw the sun high in the sky that I realized we'd missed breakfast. Uh-oh, a punishable offense in our house.

6

Travis had both skunks in the cage by the time I got back to the barn. The larger one was nosing and cuddling the smaller one, which looked frighteningly weak. I explained Dr. Pritzker's advice and then cast around for something I could use to warm the runt. I grabbed a brick from a stack and then ran with it to the back door of our house.

Our cook, Viola, sat at the kitchen table drinking a cup of coffee and taking a short break between cooking our family's huge breakfast and cooking our family's huge lunch. "You two done missed out. Your mama's not happy about that. She wants to see you."

Drat. Now I was in trouble, and I didn't have *time* to be in trouble.

"What you doing with that brick?"

Viola doted on Idabelle, our one Inside Cat, whose job it was to keep the mice at bay, so I decided to stick with the kitten story. "I need it to warm one of the barn kittens that's sick." I opened the stove and pushed the brick in, nearly burning my fingers.

"Okay, but your mama wants to see you."

I smoothed down my hair, straightened my pinafore, and marched into the parlor where Mother sat mending a big basket of my brothers' shirts. (It turns out that a passel of brothers aren't just hard on their sister; they're hard on their shirts as well.)

"Ah," said Mother, "the missing

daughter has returned. Where were you at breakfast? And where is Travis?"

The sick kitten story seemed to be holding up well, so I went on with it and then explained about having to run to Dr. Pritzker's for emergency advice. Mother didn't much like me hanging around his office, saying it wasn't a suitable place for a young lady, but she, like everyone else, felt sorry for the so-called sick kitten. She finally let me go with a word of warning not to miss any more meals, then said, "Send Travis to see me."

"I think he's still busy with our, uh, patient."

"Well then, after that. You may go."

I went back to the kitchen, took a dish towel from a drawer, and scooped out the brick and wrapped it up, again nearly burning myself. This skunk-doctoring business was dangerous in ways I hadn't expected.

I hurried out to the barn with my warm bundle.

Travis stood in the gloom next to the cage, looking anxious and biting his nails.

"Stop that," I said. "Mother will get all over you about it, and you're already in trouble for missing breakfast. Look here, I've got a way to warm the kit up."

51

"You didn't tell her we have skunks, did you?"

I marveled at the boy. Was he insane? "I told her we had a sick kitten. I told Viola that too. So that's what we've got, right?"

"Right."

We opened the cage and put the brick between the two. The bigger kit immediately nestled up beside it. The smaller one didn't quite get it, so I picked it up and put it on top of the brick. It rooted around feebly, looking like it was trying to nurse in the fuzzy towel.

"All right," I said. "Next, the warm milk. Go and find Flossie—we won't need much."

"She's out in the pasture."

"Doesn't matter. We only need a couple of squirts. I've got to find a bottle that's small enough. Or a sponge. Ugh, I guess I have to go back into the house again."

Travis grabbed an empty jar and

went out looking for our milk cow. I went back to the house, trying to think what I could use. We'd hand raised orphaned lambs and piglets with bottles in the past but they were far too big for the kit.

Viola was gone from the kitchen. I rustled around in the pantry but there was nothing we could use.

"Think, Calpurnia, think," I muttered. Somewhere in my distant past, I'd seen a tiny little bottle in the house, but where? Then it came to me.

Mother was still sewing in the parlor, so I crept quietly up the stairs so as not to attract her attention. I went into the trunk room, stacked high with wicker traveling trunks, and then up the rickety stairs into the attic. The reek of mothballs grew stronger as I climbed higher. The hatchway into the attic creaked ominously as I pushed it open. Just like in a ghost story.

Oh stop, I told myself. You're just being silly.

The attic was dark and piled high with winter quilts. My grandfather's war uniform hung from one of the rafters like a dead Confederate soldier, complete with sword. I shuddered and wished I'd brought a candle with me. In the corner stood our old rocking horse, paint chipped off, scraggly real horsehair mane and tail mostly missing from hard use by many children, including me. All seven of us had outgrown it, but for some reason Mother had not been able to pitch it out.

Over there were my old dolls sitting in a row, dolls I hadn't played with in years. They grinned at me in the gloom and spoke in a whispery chorus: "Calleeeee. Where have you been, Calleeeee? We used to be your dearest friends, but now you have abandoned

us in the dark. What do you have to say
for yourself, Calleeeee?"

I cleared my throat. "Be quiet. You're
not really talking. It's just my imagination. My *overactive* imagination."

"Are you sure, Calleeeee?"

I told myself, Calpurnia, get a grip.
I said to the dolls, "Oh, shut up."

And they did.

I opened a tin box full of doll clothes.

Buried at the bottom was a tiny glass bottle with a rubber tip. Ha! I congratulated myself on being a clever girl and skedaddled out of there before the dolls could accuse me again. I'd outgrown them and felt a bit sad about it, but not too sad because now I had other, better things in my life. Now I had my Scientific Notebook and Granddaddy to do experiments with; now I had Dr. Pritzker to teach me about animals. Now I had tadpoles that turned into frogs, caterpillars that grew into butterflies.

I crept back through the house and ran into Viola peeling spuds in the kitchen.

"What you got there?" she said, squinting at me.

"Nothing," I said, and thrust the bottle into my pinafore pocket.

"Huh. Every time you got 'nothing,' it never turns out good."

"Ha ha, very funny." I kissed her cheek and ran out before she could swat me away.

Back at the barn I waited for Travis and worried about the runt, staring at it closely to make sure it was still breathing. It lay on the brick where I'd placed it, its rib cage barely moving in tiny shallow puffs.

Travis clattered in, carrying the jar

with a couple of inches of milk. He looked like he'd been in a fistfight, with his hair standing on end and streaks of cow manure all over him.

I stared at him. "What happened to you?"

"It's Flossie," he panted. "She's not used to being milked at this time of day. She didn't like it one bit." He wiped his brow. "And all this time I thought we were friends. Did you find a bottle?"

I showed him the doll bottle, and we both agreed it was perfect. It had to be—it's all there was. I poured the warm milk into it while Travis took the runt and cuddled it in his arms.

"I think the brick is working," he said. "He feels nice and toasty."

I had my doubts. The poor thing looked pretty limp. I held the bottle to its mouth but it didn't move.

"What's wrong?" said Travis. "Why won't he drink?"

"I don't know. Maybe it won't drink cow's milk. Maybe it will only drink skunk's milk. Maybe we have to round up a skunk to milk."

But Travis was in no mood for joking. "We can't milk a skunk," he cried, sounding dangerously close to tears.

"All right then, we're going to have to force it." I squeezed the rubber tip of

the bottle, and a little milk oozed out. "Wake it up."

"How?"

"Poke it, shake it, do something."

He poked it gently but it didn't move.

All right, Calpurnia, I told myself, drastic times call for drastic measures. I pinched the kit by the scruff and pulled its head all the way back so that its tiny pink mouth gaped open. I pushed the bottle deep inside. The kit gagged, and milk dribbled down its chest.

"It won't swallow," Travis said miserably.

What more could we do? By now I figured it was a goner, and we were going to have to make yet another trip to the sad little cemetery out back where my brother's failed pets were laid to rest. Travis was just going to have to get used to it. Besides, one baby skunk should be enough for any boy, right? (Although one certain boy would never see it that way.)

And then something wonderful happened: The runt twitched its tiny nose. Then it licked its chops. Then it feebly tried to lick its fur where the milk had splattered. Signs of life!

I gave it some more milk, and it managed to swallow a couple of drops. Just a couple. But it was a start. Travis lit up like the sun, making it all worthwhile.

If Travis was an idiot to adopt two skunks, I, being one year older and so much wiser, was an even bigger idiot for going along with him, right? In my defense I have to say that I warned him and warned him, but of course he grew more and more attached to them.

So now we were stuck with (1) Stinky

the Skunk, and (2) Winky the Runt. I thanked my lucky stars there weren't a dozen kits hidden in that tree.

Dr. Pritzker came over a few days later to look at one of our pigs with an eye infection, and I hung around to watch.

"Hello, Calpurnia, how is your kitten coming along?"

"My what?"

"The kitten you told me about, the poorly one."

"Oh . . . yes, of course . . . the kitten. It's doing very well, thank you. I think your advice made all the difference."

"Would you like me to examine it after I'm done here?"

"Uh, well, perhaps some other time. I'm pretty sure it's sleeping right now, and I hate to wake it up."

Dr. Pritzker gave me a funny look but that didn't bother me. I was used to it. Lots of people gave me funny looks.

By now Stinky was eating all sorts of fruits and vegetables and bugs, along with tidbits left over from our family meals. In fact, he'd eat anything we put in front of him. Granddaddy, the source of all knowledge, explained that skunks are "omnivores," which is a

fancy way of saying they'll eat anything from popcorn to crickets to fried
chicken. One day Travis presented
Stinky with a whole pecan, which frus-
trated the kit to no end, as he was unable
to crack the thick shell with his tiny
teeth. Finally Travis cracked the nut
open for him, and Stinky greedily
inhaled the contents.

Winky was still using the bottle but
slowly improving. The hardest thing
was keeping his brick warm. We were
constantly running in and out of
the kitchen while trying not to
draw too much attention
to ourselves.

One day Travis and I walked into the barn and heard a terrible racket. We ran to the back, where Ajax, Father's prize bird dog, was barking and pawing at the skunk cage. Stinky and Winky growled back at him from the far corner, doing their best to look large and fierce.

"No, Ajax!" we screamed, but he was too excited by the presence of not just one captive varmint but *two* of them. He must have figured this was his lucky day.

I grabbed him by the collar and pulled him away, but he fought me like a wild thing and jerked loose.

Stinky stamped his feet.

"Nooo!" I cried.

Stinky turned his back.

"Nooooo!" I cried.

Stinky let fly.

Ajax took a direct hit in the face. He howled and pitched over backward, pawing at his muzzle and uttering

horrible screeches. The poor dog
screamed and thrashed as if he were
being tortured (which, if you think
about it, he was).

Travis and I could only stand there
with our mouths open, staring at this
terrible and ridiculous scene.

When Father got home from work,
Ajax was lying in his favorite place on
the front porch. Reeking. You could
smell him from miles away.

Father glared at the dog. "You, sir!
Get off the porch! You're banished for
a week. Don't come back until you've
improved."

Ajax flattened himself and slunk

away, looking very embarrassed. Unfortunately he went to his second-favorite place, which was *under* the porch, and although we could no longer see him, it turned out to be not a whole lot better, nose-wise.

Father turned on us. "You two. Do you know anything about this?"

Travis said, "Well, we—"

I elbowed him. "No, sir," I said.

"No, sir," Travis echoed. Father scowled at us. We stared at our boots.

"Pfaw!" he said, and strode into the house.

"What do we do now?" said Travis.

"I guess we better wash Ajax," I said glumly.

"Ugh."

"Exactly."

I knew that plain old water would not fix the stench.

"Stay here," I said. "I'm going to talk to Granddaddy." I went inside and knocked on the door of the library, where he spent much of his time.

He called out, "Enter if you must." He said that because he preferred to be left alone. He preferred to live what he called A Life of the Mind. This meant that he liked to sit quietly, and read lots of books, and think about things. So what kinds of things did he think about? Everything, as far as I could tell: birds, dinosaurs, fossils, volcanoes, tornadoes, the weather, the planets, the stars. I hadn't yet come across anything he hadn't thought about. I hoped he'd given some thought to skunks and dogs.

"Granddaddy, what's the best way to get the smell of skunk off a dog?"

"Ah, I take it one of the dogs has had a mishap with the family Mephitidae?"

"Yep, a mishap right in the face. He's pretty miserable. And to make it worse, Father has banished him, which makes him *really* miserable."

"Then I suggest you mix up five parts hydrogen peroxide, five parts baking soda, and one part liquid soap. Leave it on the beast for several minutes before washing it off. Repeat this process several times. You will find what you need in the laboratory."

"Thank you." I turned to go.

"Be careful not to spill the hydrogen peroxide on your clothes."

"Why?"

"It will bleach them. And avoid storing the mixture in a closed bottle."

"Why?"

"It is likely to explode."

"*Explode?* Really? Perhaps you could, uh, come and help me."

"Calpurnia, did I not teach you your proper weights and measures?"

"Yessir, you did."

"Well, then." He went back to his reading.

I went to the laboratory out back, which was really just an old shed where Granddaddy did his experiments. Sometimes I'd sit with him and take notes.

There were many bottles of chemicals on the shelves, the more dangerous ones marked with a skull and crossbones. I finally found what I needed

and measured out the three ingredi-
ents, careful to keep the mixture off
my dress. I poured it all into a big jar
and left the cap off. An explosion was
the very last thing I needed (although it
might be quite interesting). Then I
stopped off in the house and swiped
a bar of Mother's fancy rose-scented

soap that she kept for special occasions. I figured this occasion was special enough.

I met up with Travis, and we took Ajax to the river on a leash, me carrying the open jar and taking care not to spill it. Progress was slow.

Travis asked, "Why didn't you put a lid on it?"

"You don't want to know."

At the river we took off our boots and led Ajax into the water. We covered him with our recipe and made him stand there for several minutes. Then we splashed him with water and rinsed him off. Then we did it again. And again. He kept trying to climb up the bank, and we kept scolding him and pushing him back into the water. Nobody, neither child nor dog, enjoyed themselves.

Then we did a final scrub with Mother's fancy soap. Ajax still smelled like a skunk but not as much. And now he at least smelled like a skunk that had been rolling in rose petals.

"What do we do with Stinky and Winky?" Travis said.

"We'll let them go where you found them. They'll be happier in the wild, you know."

"That's not what I meant."

"Come on, Travis. . . ."

"No, Callie, not yet. Maybe when they're bigger and can look after themselves. What about Ajax? I'm afraid he'll attack them again."

"After that? No dog could possibly be that dumb."

We looked over at Ajax, who had chosen that exact second to scratch himself with such a silly expression that we both had a moment of doubt. He squinted and grinned, his upper lip caught on an eyetooth. I'd be willing to bet that no dog in the history of the world had ever looked dumber.

"Hmm," I said, "I guess we should put the kits in the loft for now. They'll be safe there."

We took Ajax home and pushed him under the porch, giving him strict instructions to "Stay!" Then we went to the loft, which was sunny and warm and dry. It smelled of sweet hay, and when the sun shone in at just the right angle, you could see a million golden flecks of dust dancing in the air. It felt like a magical place. Up there you could see all the way to the cotton gin downtown and miles of cotton fields in the other direction. It was also a good place to do gymnastics in that you could do rolls and flips and cartwheels in the loose hay without hurting yourself too badly.

It was no easy task hauling the cage up the ladder but we finally managed. Travis took the kits up in his overalls. We let them snuffle and nose around for a while and then tucked them back in their cage. We dumped a bit of loose hay over the cage to disguise it, just in case any of the other brothers came by.

The kits seemed happy in the loft. Travis brushed their fur and gave them baths and brought them little toys that they tossed about just like regular kittens. He sneaked them out for walks in the woods at dawn and at dusk, and he carried them around in the bottom of his satchel where they curled up happily enough in two black-and-white balls.

Stinky and Winky never sprayed him. They never even stamped their feet in warning. They became such beloved pets that I think Travis lost sight of the fact that his furry friends were, in fact, skunks.

I joined him in the loft every few days, still trying to convince him to let them go just as soon as they reached a certain size.

But then came the fateful morning when Winky would not play with his toys, and worse, he would not eat.

Travis looked worried at breakfast. When I asked him if there was anything wrong, he whispered, "No, I'm fine."

But I knew him better than anyone, and I could tell he was not fine. If he'd told me his plan, there's no doubt I would have talked—or maybe yelled—some sense into him. But I didn't know about it until it was too late.

I set off to school with Travis and two of my other brothers, Sul Ross and Lamar. Travis had his book satchel over his shoulder but, strangely, he was carrying his books under his arm. I was about to ask him about this when I heard someone calling my name. Up ahead, my friend Lula Gates waited for me, waving and calling.

"Hi, Lula!" I waved. I ran ahead to meet her, and we chatted all the way to school. I didn't give Travis another thought. At least, not right at that second.

We made it to school just in time to line up while Miss Harbottle rang the handbell. We trooped in, the girls in one line and the boys in the other. Our school had only one classroom, so the little ones sat up front and practiced their ABCs; the older children sat in the middle and recited their times tables; the oldest children sat in the back and studied world geography with the atlas and the globe.

Lula and I shared a desk right behind Travis, who, for some reason, looked extra fidgety. You'd have thought the boy had ants in his pants the way he kept squirming in his seat and fiddling around with the satchel at his feet.

At recess we all ran outside. Usually Travis hung around and bothered me and Lula while we played hopscotch, but this time he took his satchel to the far side of the playground. Now I knew for sure something was wrong with him, and I'd have to tell Mother. Which meant she'd either dose him with a teaspoon of cod-liver oil, the most awful substance in the entire world, or haul him off to see Dr. Walker, with his cold hands and even colder instruments.

Both prospects were enough to make you shudder.

Miss Harbottle rang the bell to signal the end of recess, and we all went back to our desks.

"Boys and girls," she said, "today we will all have a lesson in Texas history. You little ones, pay attention now. Did you know that before Texas became part of the United States, it was actually a part of Mexico? That's right, part of another country. And the brave Texians, as they were called, your very own ancestors, fought a war against Mexico to gain their independence."

Normally such a discussion would

have deeply interested Travis, but now he was busy trying to slide a box of raisins out of his desk without making any noise.

Miss Harbottle said, "The Texians suffered terrible defeats at the Alamo and at Goliad."

She pulled down the map of the United States and tapped it with her pointer to show us the sites of the famous battles. The Alamo was only fifty miles from our house. But because it was a full day's journey on the train, none of my brothers or I had seen it.

"But the tide turned at the Battle of

San Jacinto on April 21, 1836. That's where our own General Sam Houston led his ragged army of volunteers against the much larger Mexican forces commanded by General Santa Anna."

Then something happened that made the hair on the back of my neck stand up: Travis's satchel moved. On its own. Which satchels aren't supposed to do.

The flap lifted an inch, then fell shut. Then it lifted a couple of inches and fell shut. It lifted a third time and, to my horror, out poked a pointy black muzzle with twitching whiskers.

Miss Harbottle grew louder as she got to the exciting parts of the battle.

Then to my double horror, another, smaller black muzzle poked out beside the first one. The mind reeled. I couldn't believe it.

"Travis," I hissed, "what have you done?"

"Huh?"

"You can't bring skunks to school."

He looked down just in time to stop them making their escape. He gently nudged them back with his foot. I glanced around. Nobody seemed to have noticed. All eyes were on Miss Harbottle.

I whispered, "Have you lost your mind?"

He turned halfway in his chair and murmured, "Winky stopped eating. I couldn't just leave him at home; he's way too skinny. I'm trying to tempt his appetite with raisins. Normally he's a real raisin hog, but for some reason he won't eat them."

"But both? You had to bring them *both*?"

A couple of students glared at us.

"I couldn't separate them. They get so upset."

"You get them out of here right now."

Lula elbowed me to be quiet.

I thought fast and hard. Maybe I could scoop up the satchel and run for the door. And keep running all the way back to the barn. But what would Miss Harbottle say about my behavior? I'd have to plead illness. And what would my parents do? It would mean the cod-liver oil or the doctor. Was it worth it? To save Travis from his overwhelming love of animals and his own incredibly stupid decision?

I weighed my choices.

Miss Harbottle said, "General Houston led his soldiers on their surprise attack, crossing the high grass fields around the Mexican camp. General Santa Anna was so confident of victory that he had not posted any sentries to keep watch during their afternoon siesta. The Texians were only yards away when they opened

fire, shouting, 'Remember the Alamo! Remember Goliad!'"

She jumped and screamed at the top of her lungs: "*Eeeeeeee!*"

We all jumped along with her.

She ran to the corner for the broom

and held it up before her like a rifle.
Gosh! Her re-enactment was so vivid
and thrilling. Why couldn't all our les-
sons be like this? Instead of droning
on about five times five—

"Skunks!" she yelled. "Skunks!"

I looked down. Stinky and Winky were scurrying between the desks and heading right for her.

She might as well have yelled "Bomb!" for the effect it had. Piercing screams filled the air. The students erupted in panic. They started rushing for the door and dropping books and knocking over chairs.

"Travis," I yelled, "*do* something."

"Do? What should I do?"

"*Get* them."

Stinky had made it to Miss Harbottle's desk, where he hunkered down underneath in safety. Winky, slower and confused by the noise, didn't get there in time. Miss Harbottle jabbed him with the broom and moaned, "Go away, you. Oh, please go away."

"No, don't," pleaded Travis, "please don't upset them."

I also could have told Miss Harbottle that upsetting a skunk was not the best course of action and that she should just stay calm and be still, but she was from the big city of Austin and had never had to face down multiple skunks before. She took a swipe at Winky and sent him skidding into the corner.

"Oh no," said Travis, but a second

later Winky got up and shook himself. He didn't look hurt, but he didn't look happy, either. He raised his tail.

Uh-oh.

He stamped his tiny feet.

Oh no.

Miss Harbottle backed away, but just then Stinky emerged from under the desk, trapping her between them.

I called out, "Try to stay calm, Miss Harbottle."

Travis begged again, "Please don't rile them." He crept forward with his satchel. "If you'll just stay calm, I think I can get them."

She looked at him as if he were crazy. "Stay back! They're wild."

"Actually," he said, "they're—"

"Yes, Travis," I shouted, "they're wild. Can't you see how wild they are?"

Travis crept closer. Stinky advanced on Miss Harbottle. She took a swing at him and missed. He stamped his feet. But Winky beat him to it, letting loose a poof of mist from his hind end that settled on the floor and the blackboard.

"Noooo," shrieked Miss Harbottle.

Stinky turned his back to her and raised his tail. He was only four feet away. It would be a direct hit. Except that at the very second he fired, Travis launched himself through the air like a flying human shield, saving our teacher from the spray.

Coughing and gagging, we stumbled to the door and pitched down the steps into the fresh air. Travis reeked to high heaven. His streaming eyes were bright red. The other children backed away from him as fast as they could, which was just as well, since he then did the only thing he could possibly do to make things worse. He bent over and put his hands on his knees and threw up his breakfast.

Stinky and Winky scampered away in the confusion and were never seen again.

Mother ended up burning Travis's shirt. And for a while he had to eat his meal on the back porch with no company except for the dog Ajax.

Thus ended the episode of the "wild" skunk invasion of the Fentress School. Travis, who was entirely at fault for the whole thing, ended up a total disgrace in my eyes but a hero to our teacher and all our classmates. You see, because the classroom smelled so horrible, the school had to be closed and we were let out early for summer vacation.

If anyone had asked me, I could have told them that swabbing down the floor and blackboard with a mixture of five parts hydrogen peroxide, five parts baking soda, and one part soap would have fixed things well enough so that we *could* have held classes for that last week.

But no one asked me.

And I didn't bother to tell.

SKUNKED!